O'BRIEN **panda cubs**

PANDA CUBS SERIES
where reading begins

O'BRIEN SERIES FOR YOUNG READERS

 panda cubs

 pandas

 panda tales

 flyers

Emma Says Boo!

Words: Anna Donovan
Pictures: Woody Fox

THE O'BRIEN PRESS
DUBLIN

First published 2003 by The O'Brien Press Ltd,
12 Terenure Road East, Rathgar, Dublin 6, Ireland
Tel: +353 1 4923333; Fax: +353 1 4922777
E-mail: books@obrien.ie
Website: www.obrien.ie
Reprinted 2007.

ISBN: 978-0-86278-795-0

2 3 4 5 6 7 8 9 10
07 08 09 10 11 12

British Library Cataloguing-in-Publication Data
Emma says boo. - (Solo ; 3)
1.Fear - Juvenile fiction 2.Children's stories
I.Title II.Woody
823.9'14[J]

The O'Brien Press receives assistance from

the arts
council
schomhairle
ealaíon

Typesetting, layout, editing: The O'Brien Press Ltd
Printing: Leo Paper Products Ltd China

Can YOU spot the
panda cub
hidden in the story?

Emma was sleepy.
Peter was sleepy too.

'Time for bed,' said Dad.

'Goodnight, Dad,'
said Peter.
He went
upstairs.

'Goodnight, Dad,'
said Emma.

She checked in the hall
to see if there was
anything **hiding** there.

She checked the stairs.

She checked the landing.

She checked ...

'BOO!'

Peter leapt out
from his bedroom.
**He was wearing
a mask.**

Emma jumped.

Emma screamed.

Emma
shrieked.

'DAD!"

17

Peter was pleased.
He smiled.

'Goodnight, Em,'
he said.

And he shut his
bedroom door.

Bang!

Emma sobbed
and sobbed.

But at last
she went to sleep.

Next night,
Peter waited
behind the
bathroom door.

21

Emma went up the stairs.
She checked **every corner**.

She checked the landing.

She checked Peter's
bedroom door.
It was closed.

'Is it safe?' called Dad.

'Yes,' called Emma.

She went into her room.
She put on her pyjamas.

She went to the bathroom
to brush her teeth.

'Boo!'

Emma jumped.
Teddy jumped.

Teddy jumped very high!

Peter laughed
and laughed.

Dad came running.
'Not again!' he said.

'It's not fair,' said Emma.
'Peter's mean. I hate him.'

'You must make a plan,'
said Dad.

Emma sat up in her bed.
She was thinking.

She was thinking about
scaring Peter.

Next night, Emma
whispered to Dad.
He winked.

'Don't let the **fleas bite!**' said Emma.

Peter hid behind the door of the spare room.

He was wearing a sheet.

He heard Emma
coming up the stairs.

He waited
until she was
at the top.
He pounced.

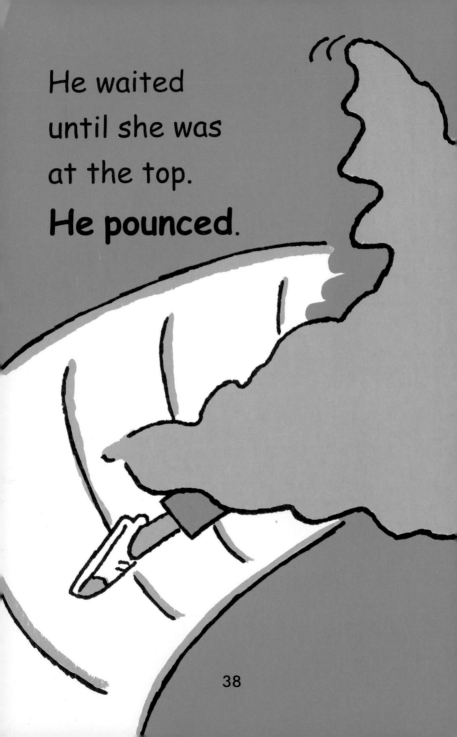

But it wasn't Emma.

It was ...

A HUGE GHOST.

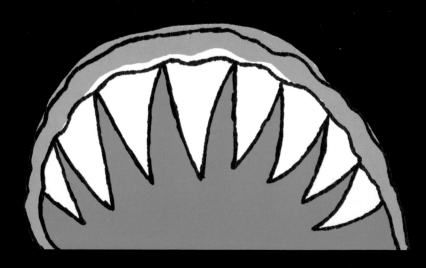

The ghost chased Peter

down the stairs.

43

'Dad, Dad!'
screamed Peter.
'Pete, what's up?'
said Dad.

'Ghost!' said Peter.

Emma took off
her sheet.

She took the tall hat
off her head.

She put down
the big sticks
she had in her hands.

'Boo!'

she said.